Dance
to the Rescue

by Laura Driscoll
based on the original teleplay by Eric Weiner
illustrated by Dave Aikins

Published by Advance Publishers, L.C.
Maitland, FL 32751 USA
www.advancepublishers.com
Produced by Judy O Productions, Inc.
Designed by SunDried Penguin

Printed in China

ISBN 1-57973-313-1

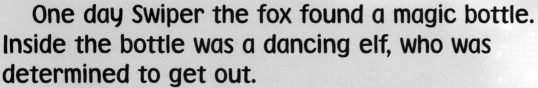

One day Swiper the fox found a magic bottle. Inside the bottle was a dancing elf, who was determined to get out.

"Maybe I can trick this fox into freeing me!" the Elf said to himself. He knew that whoever opened the bottle would be magically pulled inside to take his place.

So the Elf begged Swiper to let him out. "I need lots of room to dance!" he said.

"Aw, poor guy," said Swiper. "He's stuck in there."

So Swiper opened the bottle. *Poof!* The Dancing Elf was free—but now Swiper was trapped inside!

Then the Elf went dancing off into the forest, leaving Swiper all alone.

"Oh Mannn!" moaned Swiper. "I need help. Maybe Dora and Boots can help me."

Swiper made his way to Dora and Boots and told them how the Dancing Elf had tricked him. "And now I'm stuck in here!" he cried.

"You poor fox," said Dora.
She started to open the bottle, but Swiper stopped her.
"If you open the bottle, *you'll* go in," he warned.
"Don't worry," Dora said. "We'll find a way to
get you out of this bottle. I promise."

Just then the bottle began to shake. It was dancing—and singing, too! The bottle told Dora, Boots, and Swiper that they would have to win one big wish.

"Where can we win one big wish?" asked Boots.

"If you make it to the Castle and win the King's dance contest, you'll win one big wish!" the bottle explained. "Then you could wish Swiper out of the bottle!"

Dora, Boots, and Swiper set off for the Castle right away. To get there, first they had to get through the Pyramid, which was guarded by the red Marching Ants. They wouldn't let Dora, Boots, and Swiper pass until they marched like Marching Ants.

 Will *you* help Dora, Boots, and Swiper march like Marching Ants? March, march, march!

The Ants were impressed—and they let Dora, Boots, and Swiper pass!

Farther along the path some Wiggling Spiders blocked their way. They wouldn't let Dora, Boots, and Swiper through until they wiggled like Wiggling Spiders . . .

 Wiggle your elbows! Wiggle your wrists! Dance like a Wiggling Spider!

. . . and the Spiders let them pass.

Finally Dora, Boots, and Swiper met up with some Sneaky Snakes. The Snakes wouldn't let them pass until they danced like snakes.

So Dora, Boots, and Swiper slithered and slid like the Sneaky Snakes . . .

 Put your hands over your head! Move them side to side! Slither like a Sneaky Snake!

and the Snakes let them pass. They made it through the Pyramid!

Next Dora, Boots, and Swiper made their way to the Ocean. There they met up with the Pirate Pig and his Pirate Piggies.

"We need to sail across the Ocean to win one big wish and free Swiper," Dora explained to them.

The Pirate Pig was happy to give them a ride across the Ocean on his pirate ship. But as they sailed, the waves got bigger and bigger. Suddenly a big wave washed Swiper and the magic bottle overboard! Before Dora could reach the bottle, a whale came up for air and—*gulp!*—he swallowed the magic bottle—Swiper and all!

Luckily, Backpack was carrying something that could make the whale sneeze: pepper!

"Ah-choo!" The whale sneezed a big sneeze. The bottle flew out of the whale's blowhole and back to safety on the pirate ship.

"That was fun!" Swiper said with a laugh. "I've never been sneezed by a whale before!"

As they sailed on, a Stormy Storm rolled in. The only way the Stormy Storm would let the ship pass was if everyone aboard did the Pirate Dance.

"That's our special dance!" said Pirate Pig. He and the Pirate Piggies started to dance, and Dora and Boots joined in . . .

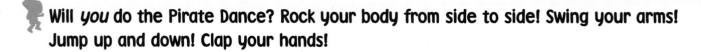

Will *you* do the Pirate Dance? Rock your body from side to side! Swing your arms! Jump up and down! Clap your hands!

. . . and the Stormy Storm let them pass! They made it to the Castle just in time for the King's dance contest.

But the guard wouldn't let Dora and Boots into the Castle. "You have to wear fancy clothes!" he told them. "King's rules!"

Just then Benny floated by in his hot-air balloon with a bow tie for Boots and a fancy gown for Dora.

Dora and Boots were ready to dance! But the Dancing Elf was at the contest too. He wanted to win the one big wish for himself. And he *was* a good dancer!

King Juan el Bobo started the contest. "First you must do my favorite dance," he said. "The 'Ants in Your Pants' dance!"

Dora, Boots, and Swiper wiggled their hips like they had ants in their pants. So did the Dancing Elf.

 Help Dora and Boots win the contest! Wiggle your hips like you have ants in your pants!

The King laughed. "Oh, that was very good," he told the dancers. But he wasn't ready to name a winner. He had another silly dance he wanted them to do. "To win one big wish," he said, "next you must dance like a fish!"

So everyone danced like a fish. They made fish faces. They flapped their arms like fish fins.

 Let's see *your* fish face! Flap your arms like fish fins!

"*¡Excelente!*" said King Juan el Bobo. "You were all so good. I still can't pick a winner."

So the King gave the dancers the hardest challenge of all. "You must get my mommy to dance," he said. The King was sad that his mommy never danced.

"I'm just not good at it," said the King's mommy.

Dora had an idea. "We can do the 'Everyone Can Dance' dance," she said.

"Yeah," said Boots. "That dance gets *everyone* dancing!"

So Dora, Boots, and Swiper did the "Everyone Can Dance" dance!

Soon everyone was dancing—even the King's mommy!

Help get the King's mommy to dance! Do the "Everyone Can Dance" dance. Put your hands on your hips! Shake your hips! Clap your hands! Jump up and down!

"You've done it!" said the King. "You got my mommy to dance! So I will give you one big wish! What do you wish for?"

Dora smiled. "I know what to wish for," she said. "I wish Swiper free!"

 Help Dora's wish come true. Say "I wish Swiper free!"

Poof! In a swirl of sparkles Swiper was free!

The Dancing Elf was sorry that he tricked Swiper.

"I guess I have to go back into the bottle," he said sadly.

Dora asked the King if the Dancing Elf could stay out of the bottle. "He really loves to dance, and there's no room in there," she pointed out.

The King agreed—and declared that the Dancing Elf was
to be free of the bottle forever! Everyone was thrilled.
And do you know what they did to celebrate?
They danced!